A WEE DRIBBLE OF DROSS

by
Walter McCorrisken
(semi-skilled poet)

Birlinn

© Walter McCorrisken, 1993

Published by
Birlinn Ltd,
13 Roseneath Street,
Edinburgh

Typeset in Times,
and printed and bound in
Great Britain by
Cox & Wyman Ltd, Reading

A CIP record for this book
is available from the British Library

ISBN 1 874744 12 2

FOREWORD

THE POET

Beauty, though to others hidden,
Is revealed to the poet in town and midden.
God's gift to him, to others concealed,
Shows the Almighty keeps his eyes peeled.

DOOMED TO BE A POET

When people say to me that they do not
understand poetry, they worry unjustly
and apologize.

I say unto them I do not understand potatoes
but I eat them just the same. It depends on
the approach.

When I first tried to understand potatoes I
studied them for hours! Since then I enjoy
potatoes but no longer try to understand them.
In fact, sometimes I enjoy poetry and potatoes
at the same time. It hasn't affected me in any way.

This life to me is full of fun,
Of drama and adventures.
How oft the unexpected cough,
Precedes the flying dentures?

SCOTIA !

Oh Scotia, Scotia,
I see you in my dreams,
Thy bonnie purple heather,
Thy rushing, peaty streams.
And the bonnie lassies
With their milking pail.
But hark! a forgotten coo
Gives a plaintive wail!

Oh Scotia, Scotia,
In my dreams I see my hoose once mair,
The child playing with its brethren.
On the clean but muddy flair.
And Granny guarding the Jelly Pan,
Skelping wasps right aff her belly.
They were attracted by the succulent smell
Of her lovely bramble jelly.

Oh many were the cheery nights,
Friends gathered from afar,
To drink the Elderberry wine
And count tadpoles in a jar.
Oh Scotia, tho' you're far away,
My heart's still jerking madly,
When I think of yon happy days,
But sadly, oh how sadly!

Oh Scotia, Scotia,
Wert I in yonder glen,
To hear the sound of porridge
Being ett by sturdy Highland men.
Anyway, Scotia, I'll ne'er forget
Your hilly land with more than one river,
I'll never forget you, never ever!

LIMERICKS

A wumman who was chewing a caramel,
Was spoke to by a wise, old camel.
"You've got two humps," grunted he,
"So I take it to be,"
"Like a camel you're some kind of mammal?"

A nasty old man from North Hantz,
Was fond of dropping his pantz.
Now in his cell each dawn,
He sitz most forlorn,
Holding his head in his hantz.

A weird old man of Calcutta,
Repaired his roof with choice butta.
When the sun shone too hot,
It melted the lot,
And the butta flowed all down the gutta.

A gourmet named round-belly Nick,
Ate cheese with a sharp pointed stick.
He could eat up the cheese
With elegant ease,
But a plum cake required a pick.

A remarkable man from Renfrew,
Kept peas on a knife with strong glue.
Because they were gummy
The peas stuck to his tummy,
But, sadly the knife stuck there, too.

There was an old man of Coblenz,
Who refused to pay the high renz.
The enraged landlord,
Threatened him with a sword,
Now the family's living in tenz.

A foolish old man of Traquair,
Couldn't find his legs anywhere.
He said in dismay,
"They were here yesterday."
He was sitting on them in a chair.

A troubled old man of Tashkent,
Somehow got both his knees bent.
He said with great zest,
"One foot points to the west,
But the other, I can't see where it went."

A farmer from County Kildare,
Kept a swallow and a pet hare.
He was elated when both his pets mated,
And the result's in the air, a pet sware.

A fat Scotsman name of McSkinner,
Decided to cut down on dinner.
He ate the part of a coo
Known as the "moo",
Now McSkinner's quite a lot thinner.

A Scotsman named Angus MacFadyen,
Was reviled far and wide as a bad yin.
For, unknown to his spouse,
When out of the house,
He had a habit of cadgin'.

A Scot near the mighty Cairngerms,
Was infested by nasty woodwerms.
Through the holes in the walls,
With relief he now calls,
"I'm glad it's not Pachyderms!"

A thirsty wee man from Stranraer,
Was too fond of a jaer in a baer.
He went home late one night,
His wife gave him a fright,
For a pint he'll show you the scaer.

A wee grocer in down town Carnoustie,
Sold cheese that was rather foustie.
Noo he's in Jile,
Long years to beguile,
Through bars exceedingly roustie .

A model who lived in Kirkcaldy,
Was renowned for her bonnie, wee baldy,
But a revealing new gown,
Caused her mother to frown,
Who thought her daughter looked galdy.

A gardener who lived near Milngavie,
Grew onions at least four foot havie,
And for miles around,
Came a low, sobbing sound,
From passers-bavie wiping their avie.

There was an old man of Lochgelly,
Who ate onions with green table-jelly.
Said he with a sigh.
"It brings tears to my eye,"
But strangely never harms my belly.

DOWN BUT NOT TRODDEN

Some people treat me with disdain,
As if I were a Yorkie and they a Great Dane.
Folk do not give me a second glance,
And when they do it's with askance.
They think I'm just an unlettered oaf,
And wouldn't give me tuppence to help buy a loaf.

They grudge me the price of four hen eggs,
To stimulate and nourish my elderly legs.
But what care I, I'm free as an eagle,
When I walk my dog, (part Beagle).

Publishers have spurned me in a fit of peak,
But I ignore them by turning the other cheek.
They are not fit to tie my bootlaces
And can be distinguished by the egg on their faces.
I said to my friend, "They have treated me shabby."
He said, "I would use a stronger word like scabby!"

But obviously though, they have no regard,
For the sensitive feelings of a humble Bard.
They have no concept what the poor poet goes through,
Lentil soup on his semmit, beads of sweat on his broo,
As he struggles for that elusive word or phrase,
To please the masses who, if they don't like it are a dam
disgrace!

Good people, I implore, if you have a crumb of compassion,
Please help put an end to this poet bashing.

GLASGOW'S YEAR OF CULTURE

TUNE:
THE WARK O' THE WEAVERS.

CHORUS.
If it wisnae for oor culture whaur would we be?
Nae champagne for oor breakfast nae knife and fork tea,
And we'd a' be talking common, no' like you and me,
If it wisnae for this year o' culture.

There's bits o' ferm machinery hinging roosty on a wa',
That would still be lying dormant for years beneath the
straw,
This art would a' be lost tae the punters wan and a',
If it wisnae for this year o' culture.

Oor hoose is long forgotten, it's noo oor habitat,
And hinging oot the washing has become a work of art,
We can even admire fungus on an apple tart,
Thanks tae this year o' culture.

Noo Granny's in her wet suit deep in the Broomielaw,
Collecting strange objects her Granny threw awa',
You can buy them at the Barras for a grand or even twa,
Thanks tae this year o' culture.

And when we're auld and grumphy languishing at hame,
And the Culture Vultures are back tae whaur they came,
We'll be eating jeely pieces, we'll a' be oot the game,
Still peying for the year o' culture.

Edinburgh has its castle built on high,
To avoid flooding and to keep the keep and tourists feet dry,
Which is a blessing if your shoes are leaky
On a rainy day in this town called by the cunning inhabitants, "Auld Reekie".
Who well know that "Auld Reekie" is hard for the Bard to rhyme with many words, which I think is cheeky.

It is even more difficult with the word "Edinburgh",
Which to my knowledge, only rhymes with a Glasgow Father and Murra and the Glasgow Father's Brurra.
The main street is Princes Street, which is only half-finished,
With buildings on one side, which I hasten to add because of this the street is in no way diminished.

But my wish is to the brewers with all my might and main,
"May ye have long, hot summers with not a hint of rain",
For in rainy weather people tend to drink hot, steaming tea,
Which is good for the harbour master exporting tea from Trincomalee.
But it is bad news for brewers in our capital city,
Whose breweries are situated some forty miles from Glasgow, more's the pity.

For one poor Edinburgh brewer was almost driven insane,
By many months of constant drumming on his roof of very heavy rain.
And if he had lived in Paris there is no doubt he would have jumped into the Seine.

So let's think of the Edinburgh brewers because,
I think they're well worth a round of applause,

And all best wishes to those in Edinburgh, anyway'
Not forgetting the brewers, "Hip, Hip, Hooray!".

EDINBURGH

American tourists, so they say,
Can tour the world in just one day.
They sleep at night, hence this wee verse,
Or they'd attempt the universe.

EDINBURGH CASTLE

To the builders of Edinburgh Castle
We should really build a shrine.
For having the sense to build it
So near the railway line.

EDINBURGH FESTIVAL

Each year I go to the Festival,
But what really makes me mad.
They come in fur coats and nae knickers —
And the women are sometimes as bad

TOTTIEKNOWE FARM

Tak me whaur the heather growes,
Whaur the coo its turnip chows,
Whaur lives the fermer and his spouse
At Tottieknowe.

Tak me whaur the lassies bonny
Coil up wild macaroni,
Tae load upon a waiting pony
At Tottieknowe.

Tak me whaur in Highland pool
The Heron keeping wan leg cool,
Is watched by weans who've plunked the school
At Tottieknowe.

Tak me whaur the coos is grazing,
Whaur Ah think it's real amazing,
They've never heard o' double glazing
At Tottieknowe.

Tak me whaur the toad loups high
Catching each unwary fly,
Beneath the blue or azure sky
At Tottieknowe.

Tak me whaur there's room tae spare
Tae hing yer claes upon the flair,
'Cos they've only got wan chair,
At Tottieknowe.

Tak me whaur the bumbee drones
Abin the smell o' treacle scones
And the collie guards its bones
At Tottieknowe.

Tak me whaur the fermer creaks
As he bends doon in clatty breeks
Tae tend wi' care his bonny leeks
At Tottieknowe.

Tak me whaur yon piggy's brows
Remain unwrinkled as he chows,
Whaur he's content wi' willing sows
At Tottieknowe.

Tak me whaur naebuddy froons,
Whaur they eat wi' widden spoons
And gang tae bed in lang nichtgoons
At Tottieknowe.

Tak me there when Ah retire,
Tae sit and dream forenenst the byre,
Where pigs, in play, perspire in the mire
At Tottieknowe.

THE LAIRD O' PUDDOCK HALL

The young laird lay in proud array
Upon the bridal bed,
Sweaty socks wis on his feet,
A hauf bottle near his head.
He waited for his bonnie bride,
He wisnae in a hurry,
For he had sent her tae a shop
Tae bring him back a curry.

"Haste ye back," he ca'ed tae her,
"Don't forget the Mammy Mine."
He guzzled doon some venison
Then rifted like a swine.
Then his servant came a'running,
Oot fae the sma'est room,
His servant came a'running
Wi' his troosers hinging doon.

Says the servant tae his Maister,
The Laird o' Puddock Ha',
"It's yer ain true love, dear Maister,
She's went and shot the Craw.
She's gone wi' young Boy Cecil
Wi' yer siller, kye and a'.
You'll get nae Curry Supper,
For they've louped the Midden Wa'".

The Laird he galloped a' ower the land,
Scooring hoose and thicket.
He parked too lang in Glesga' Toon,
And wis landed wi' a ticket.
A' nicht lang he galloped on,
Frozen snaw upon his snout,
He sniffed a while at a chip shop door,
At the smell that floated out.

He strode intae that chip shop,
Ordered chips and a hot mince pie,
The Wench behind the coonter
Stared wi' a bloodshot eye,
For 'twas his ain true love
Frying Finnan Haddie,
"Forgive me Maister," she ca'ed oot,
"Boy Cecil is a baddie!"

She kaimed his hair, she kissed his heid,
She couldnae kiss his face,
She confided tae her closest freen',
"He disnae use toothpaste."
She kaimed his hair wi' her gowden kaim,
The five hairs oan wan oxter.
"Oh, kaim, kaim the ither wan, tae.
In vain he tried tae coax her."

Boy Cecil came up the Chip Shop stair,
Wi' fresh siller fae the Pawn.
A kerry-oot in his hunting coat,
A dumpling in each haun'.
Boy Cecil wi' his fluttering hauns,
The Laird could thole nae mair,
He struck him wi' a bunch o' fives
And hurled him doon the stair.

"Trater, T-R-A-T-E-R," he ca'ed tae him,
He wisnae good at spelling,
"Come nae mair tae Puddock Hall,
Darken not my dwelling."
Boy Cecil dived intae the Clyde,
Thoosands cried, "He'll dee."
As they sadly watched his upturned bum
Floating oot tae sea.

Noo, when auld salts hear the waves,
They'll no' fish the Firth o' Clyde,
For an icy wind blaws and freezes the Craws,
And Buoy Cecil bobs on the tide.
And tourists cry in the summer-time,
As they staun' oan Gourock Pier,
"There's a bald man in the watter,
And he's cut fae ear tae ear!"

"Don't worry," laugh the sailors,
As they drink dark, navy rum,
"It floats in wi' the tide each day,
It's only a love-sick bum."
Noo, yonder oan Gleniffer Braes,
Where stands the Puddock Ha',
The Laird and his Lady fair,
Forever sing and play fitba'.

WISHING

How high and slender the sycamore,
Were I a woman could I wish for more,
Than to have a trunk like this tall tree
And all the men chasing after me.

HORTENSE THE HEDGEHOG

There was a wee hedgehog, Hortense,
Who should have had more sense.
She fell in a puddle,
Right up to her middle,
Now she's attacked by the bends.

BRIDAL NIGHT

Breathes there a man with soul so dead,
Who never to his bride has said;
"I'm so happy, I'm so gled
To share a fish supper here in bed."

SIDEBOARD

Every house should have one,
A sideboard is a must.
It's handy for leaving messages,
Written in the dust.

THE SILVER BIRCH

It is the most gracefullest of the trees,
Because it dances like a fairy in the slightest breeze.
That is why no one in his right mind would ever besmirch,
That magnificent tree of silver, hence its name, the silver
birch .

EAGLESHAM, CONSERVATION VILLAGE

There's real coos in the meadows
A' chewing the cud,
And in spring it's right bonnie
When the trees are in bud.

And if you're gey drouthy,
To add to its charms,
There's the Swan in Polnoon Street
And the Eglinton Arms.

There's the reek of blue wood-smoke,
Fae mony a lum,
And friends at the doorstep
Are glad that you've come.

RETIREMENT

Welcome telly
And larger belly,
But goodbye feet.

PENSIONER

It's a long, cauld winter
When you're toddlin' doon the brae,
With only icy roads
Tae speed you on your way.

THE HUNGRY POET

The poet, with ease, can visualize,
Scenes of splendour with inward eye,
The mossy brook 'neath azure sky,
And when he feels hungry
Heaped beans on pie.

GRACE

The food before us upon oor plate,
Is not to be admired but there to be ate.
So let us, without no more ado,
Get tore in be it fish or coo.

GOURMET'S PRAYER

Grant me please, a brimming bowl
Of carrots and of stew,
And a healthy appetite,
Like elephants in the zoo.

BEHAVING AT BANQUET

Here are a few tips to preserve some etiquette,
When you go to a banquet where food is being ett.

A spot of dark brown, fruity sauce
Tempts the appetite and encourages the speed of human
jaws.
But take a tip from the coo as it chews the cud,
Chew your food till it resembles the constituency of mud.

This helps the food to adhere to the stomach wall
And not drop straight down — which is no good at all.
For food must linger in the body to be appreciated
And nourish the tissues before being evacuated.

And if you use the wrong spoon and don't want to appear
glaicket,
When no one's looking just wipe it on your neighbour's
jaicket.
And if his stomach rumbles and you fear he's going to
spew,
Quickly direct his head away from you.

Just follow these tips to improve your style,
And you'll never be thought more of an imbecile.

ANIMALS

SUMMER HEAT

Thigh deep in tidal waters cool,
Stand a coo, a calf and hairy bull.
As the tide flows the rising ripples
Reach right up and cool their nipples.

THE SOARING LARK

Hark ! Hark ! The soaring lark,
How powerful his pinions!
Which prevent him crashing down
On to the farmer's ingins.

WOODLAND STREAM

Where the Water Rat or Vole,
Peeps from aperture or hole,
And above the Thrush or Throstle,
Snaps the Midges as they jostle.

A GIRAFFE

It's quite a distance from his nostrils
Away down to his toes.
I often wonder late at night,
How does he pick his nose?

THE ELEPHANT

We stare at the Elephant full of awe,
Admiring the tusk on either jaw.
But what I cannot comprehend,
Is why a tail on either end?

TWO FLEAS

Two fleas met in a cheap dance hall,
Under the murky, dreary light.
One enquired of the other,
"Who's taking you home tonight?"

THE LAUGHING HYENA

This animal cannot be so bright,
It laughs all day and half the night.
I wonder would it laugh so much,
If someone kicked it in the crotch?

PEOPLE

THE ROAST CHICKEN

Four weans wanted a leg apiece,
Then faither lost the heid,
"It's just a chicken Ah'm carving,
No' a centipede!"

A HOUSEWIFE'S PRAYER

Wouldn't life be far more jolly?
Wouldn't life be just divine?
If the modern shopping trolley
Would go in one straight bliddy line!

A HUNGRY MAN

There was a hungry man,
And he ate a ploughman's lunch.
He's recovering in hospital,
From that ploughman's punch.

PET KITTEN

I found a little kitten
And kept it as a pet.
If Mummy hadn't sat on it,
I would have had it yet.

A SMALL COWBOY

A cowboy with wee legs like a dachshund,
By his pardners was treated like scum.
For they shouted to him on the prairie,
"You're only a low-down bum!"

RITA

Every time I think of Rita,
She's so nice that I could eat her.
My heart thumps madly in my vest,
Then I collapse and take a rest.

HOUSE HUNTING

"It's a low-roofed cottage," the agent said,
"Though it's really very nice."
But we had second thoughts, b'Goad,
When we saw the bow-legged mice!

PEDIGREE PET PUPPY

I gave my love a puppy,
"It's a pedigree," I said,
"It won't take much to feed it,
For the poor wee thing is dead."

WONDER

'Tis full of wonder, this world of ours,
Folk wonder at the birds and flowers.
I wonder long and wonder oft,
Why bread goes dry and biscuits soft.

A NAVAL SURGEON

"So you're a naval surgeon,"
The woman spoke in surprise.
"It's great nooadays how doctors
Tend to specialize."

A POLITICIAN

Some folk think it must be grand,
To be a politician.
But why not live off the fat of the land
By being a dietician?

DIET

A wumman chucked her diet,
And she sobbed in deep despair,
"Ah'm no' gaun tae starve tae death,
Just tae live a few years mair."

A CROOKED FISHMONGER

I knew a crooked fishmonger,
Who was cruel and a dam disgrace.
For he became a rich man,
By hammering sardines into plaice.

TOURISTS

The tourists come from far and near
To view auld Scotia's scenes.
But alas, they are restricted
By toast piled high with beans.

GUSTAV BROWN

Gustav Brown endured great pain,
Kept complaining to his brothers.
A pain he was to his family,
But a greater pain to others.

WOMEN

Women are different from us men,
Most are, in fact, superior.
Though both may look the same inside,
A woman has a more rounded exterior.

CHRISTMAS PRESENT

The scarf I got for Christmas,
It gave me such a fright,
Ah complained to the shopkeeper,
"This tartan scarf's too tight!"

NEWLY-WEDS

The newly-weds left the church,
But they werenae in a hurry.
For someone had pelted them with rice,
Fried rice and Indian curry.

MALE CHAUVINIST PIG

A chauvinist pig gave up his seat
To a bonny, blue-eyed maid.
"How come you've changed?" his wife exclaimed.
"I've cramp in my leg." he said.

A BIASED WIFE

My wife is very biased,
There is nae doot o' that.
For when we go oot shopping,
It's buy us this and buy us that.

THE BALLAD OF THE RENFREW FERRY

Welcome aboard shipmates, this elegant craft,
Although she's gey auld she's got an excellent "draught",
But before you get settled, before you get merry,
Here's a potted history of the wee Renfrew Ferry.

For years she took workers fae toons either side,
And they laboured in Singer's or built ships on the Clyde.
It was bunnets and boots and patched dungarees,
And hauf a plain loaf and a big daud o' cheese.
There was nae nautical talk like, "Man the Crow's Nest"
Or "Keel haul that stowaway stripped tae his vest!"
Thank Goad we were saved that dreadful ordeal,
For you couldnae keel haul if you hudnae a keel.

Naw, the talk was of wummen, n' horses, n' that,
And the crabbit auld Gaffer in his big bowler hat.
But whether fae the Yoker or Renfrew you came,
Baith ends o' the Ferry looked exactly the same.
You know whit Ah mean, baith ends are dead square,
For there's nae Bow or Stern tae be seen anywhere.
Wan night going hame it was such a tight squeeze,
They were packing folk in wi' a Shoehorn and Grease,

But, "Make room for wan man." the Captain implored,
"And if you breathe in we can haul him aboard."
That wee man was crushed and his ribs they were sair,
But he suffered the pain for his thoughts were elsewhere.
He hoped that his wife would have Hot Pie and Beans,
And he threatened divorce when she pit doon Sardines
But whit Ah think's tragic, whit's really a shame,
The wee Renfrew Ferry never boasted a name.

But tae be named efter a flooer or even a bird,
The wee Renfrew Ferry would consider absurd.
Like the two that replaced her, The Rose and The Swan,
You could pit them thegither in the Elderpark Pond!

You could ca' it the Matchbox, even the Gaffer, B'Goad!
Or whit's wrang wi' the Welder or the River Clyde Toad?
But name or nae name she'll be remembered wi' pride,
By the men who created bigger ships on the Clyde.
Noo the Ferry's at rest, her chains a bit roosty,
And her Captain's retired tae a Ferm near Carnoostie.

SAGA O' DA SPOOT CATCHER'S DAUGHTER

Translated from the Norse into Shetlandic/Glesga
By Waldur McErikson. (Walter McCorrisken).

Here is da saga o' da Spoot Catcher's Daughter
Who lived wi' her Faider near da green water.
Fae morn tae night in da Simmer Dim
They watched the tide geng oot and sometimes come in.
And when it wis oot they catched Spoots idda saand
By twisting a forked stick they held in their haand.

They wis watched by wee ponies whose tails reach da
grun'
And sweep up the mess they previously have done.
These toty, wee ponies is specially bred,
Their heids being near girse on which they are fed.
So they're never faur fae a meal like their big, mainland
brother,
And da wee Shetland foals coorie under their mother.

A High Heid Yin fae Glesga wi' high polished boots
Wis employed by da tax man as a coonter o' Spoots .
He catched a glimpse o' da Spoot Catcher's golden haired
daughter,
Who was feeding wee Spoots tae her peerie, pet otter.
When she fluttered her eye-lashes he blushed tae his roots,
And doomed wis that High Heid Yin, that coonter o'
Spoots.

They spent lang weekends wi' wan anidder,
Separating Spoots that wis cleppit tagidder.
When da Faider complained, "Coontin' Spoots on a Sunday?"
Da Heid Yin yelled oot, "Yer bum's oot da windae!"
And he woo'ed her and won her wi' kisses and cuddles
As they embraced on da shores of da big Shetland puddles.

They walkit barefoot ower acres o' peat
And folk admired the sun-tan on baith o' their feet.
And da Simmer Dim nights wis ideal for romancing,
Wi' a wee break at times for da Piggot dancing.
But dere's scarcely nae time even tae piddle
When dere's Piggot music coming oot o' da fiddle.

SAGA 2

He proposed in a Peerie Hoose that they should be wed,
And she shyly said, "Yes," as she bent her blond head .
But surprised wis da Heid Yin, that coonter o' Spoots
Tae see her hair wis dyed black, black at da roots.
They settled in Glesga at da famed Glesga Barras,
Where they sell juicy Spoots wi' a side dish o' Marras.

This dish fae da Shetlands that is fit for da Queen
Wis a change for the punters fae Chicken Supreme.
Whit a treat for da weans and their Murras and Farras,
Tae eat spoots oot a poke at da wonderful Barras.
Noo the Heid Yin's contented tho' a bit o' a glutton,
Being addicted tae Spoots and hot, reestit mutton.

And that is da Saga o' da Heid Yin and Wife,
Who left Shetland for Glesga and a new life.
De'il a peel she regrets whaur he has brought her,

She's happy in Glesga is da Spoot Catcher's Daughter
She's got three weans and a hoose she dichts wi' a cloot
Thanks tae the Heid Yin and a wee beast ca'ed a Spoot.

Spoot or Razor-shell. A Mollusc Bi-valve.
So named from its sword-shaped shell.

The ancient Vikings , (Spoot-guzzlers), who were not so
ancient, only appearing so by their salt-encrusted beards, were
probably the first to poke for Spoots by using the horns which
they unscrewed from their helmets.

The helmets, sans horns, were utilized as cooking pots, the
Spoots being then thrown into boiling water for a minute or so.
N.B. These horns were also popular as a cure for headache. By
placing the tip of a horn up a comrade's nostril a Vilking would
blow strongly until relief was obtained.

The sound occasioned was similar to an Alpenhorn but more
penetrating causing sheep to fly in panic until they collapsed and
died from heat exhaustion. The meat thereof was considered a
great delicacy by the Vikings who called it "Reestit Mutton" as
it was already roasted by the heat generated by the speeding
sheep.

Don't turn up da nose   Ne'er cock the snoot
At things found in da Voes.   At the humble Spoot.

ISLAND OF LUING

Luing, Luing, bonnie island of Luing,
Oh what delights thy name does bring.
The wee Cuan Ferry birling around,
Bobbing and whirling across Cuan Sound.
There's nae sherp end or blunt end, baith ends are the same,
On the wee Cuan Ferry bringing folk hame.
Aye, bringing folk hame or setting folk free,
The wee Cuan Ferry's the right boat for me.

And waiting tae greet you are the broon coos of Luing,
The famous broon coos and their prancing offspring.
And the grey seal with long neck snorts, "How do you do?",
Tae the wide-eyed tourists admiring the view.
And the cheeky, wee midges apologise first,
Before diving doon and slaking their thirst.
And the big, moth-like buzzard floats high on the wing,
Causing wee birds tae gasp and forget for tae sing.

Though there's nae streets as we know them, it's a blessing, B'Goad,
For that curious, wee beastie, the Cullipool Toad.
For there's nae traffic tae squash him, him and his mates,
As they head for the quarries wi' their female dates,
For the lonely slate quarries are fu' o' cauld watter,
If you chuck in a stane the tadpoles will scatter.
And the slates on the beach grind in the swell,
While up on the hills grows the Bog Asphodel.

There's so much tae see and so much tae do,
Tramping the wild moorlands or watching a coo.
It's so peaceful and quiet giving comfort and solace,
There's nae crowds hence nae noise and likewise nae Polis',
Ah! The still of the morning all round the coast,
Nae sound tae be heard but the scraping of toast.
And the wee Cuan Ferry keeps birling around,
Bobbing and weaving across Cuan Sound.

THE BEEF BA' BALLAD
A Border Ballad Bordering on Something.

The King cried ower the big, wide moat
That guarded the castle wa's,
"Hurry doon tae the supermart, hen,
There's wan pee aff meat ba's!"
The Queen cam oot o' the parlour
Wi' honey stuck ower her jaws,
For she had heard the King's glad cry,
"There's wan pee aff meat ba's!"

She brocht oot her bicycle
Fae the gairdener's manky shed,
And she held on tae her gowden croon
As doon the road she sped.
She ca'ed untae the wummen
Grazing coos upon the moss,
"Lift up your goons and run,
There's wan pee aff meat ba's!"

And doon the road, the stoory road,
Fae cley biggin and great ha's,
There cam a hungry multitude
A' clamouring for meat ba's.
The manager rubbed his sweaty hauns,
The registers were rid hot,
And wummen clanking past the desk,
Said, "Whit a loat we've goat."

The cashiers cried, "Wan pee aff."
As they sat upon their chair,
They werenae very cumfy,
For meat ba's were everywhere.
And they steyed beside their cash desks
For days and nights as well,
And survivors kept repeating,
"Oh, it wis a beef ba' hell!"

A wumman smiled at her braw man,
As she kaimed her gowden hair,
"Eat up a' your meat ba's, sir,
"For I have plenty mair."
Then up spake he wi' rid, rid face,
"Ah cannae eat nae mair."
"For in and oot o' these fine meat ba's
Is entwined your gowden hair."

BEEF BA' 2

The wumman laughed and showed her stumps,
She laughed richt lang and bonny,
"That's no' ma gowden hair at a'
"It's simply macaroni."
The cockerel crawed his morning sang
Through the east wind's icy blaw
And still that brave man guzzled on
Till he ett the last meat ba'.

The King cam striding ben the hoose,
Maist thocht that he would fa',
For everywhere he pit his fit
There squelched a wee meat ba'.
The deer-hounds lay a' peched oot,
It was just as he had feared,
Their bellies were like big balloons
And their legs had disappeared.

The King he was bleedin' sair,
He'd tummled ower beef ba's.
"Don't worry nane," he cried in pain,
"It's just tamata sauce."

"Aw screw the heid, your Majesty,"
Cried the loyal 10th Hussars,
"Just rub yourself wi' butter
"And you'll no' see any scars!"

And ower the toon and ower the glen
Cam lood the cries o' weans and men,
A cry sae sad and wracked wi' pain,
"Aw naw, Mother, it's no' beefy ba's again!"
And birds were fa'in' aff the trees,
They couldnae sing because
For when they stoated aff the grun'
They coughed up beefy ba's.

And wee boys piled up meat ba's,
They had stole them fae the poat,
Then they started chucking them
Right doon intae the moat.
And frogs and toads cam loupin' oot,
Oot fae the grass and weed,
It's nae fun tae have hard meat ba's
Stoatin' aff your heid.

BEEF BA' 3

Auld wummen hirplin' hame at night,
Late fae the Bingo Ha's,
Were gey shoogly and they fell
Amang these sticky ba's.
And paper boys in early morn,
Delivered the papers a' sticky and torn,
And punters who fun' the racing page
Soggy wi' sauce went mad wi' rage.

The King he acted swiftly,
Wi anger in his e'e,
"Haun' me doon that muckle quill pen
And I'll sign a high decree,
For Ah think that a' you folk,
Ah think you've got good cause,
Ah'll just have tae prohibit
The sale o' cheap meat ba's."

The King ca'ed oot the midden men,
He didnae want nae trouble,
But the midden men had plenty
Keeping meat ba's on the shovel.
And nooadays people walk aboot,
Of meat ba's there's nae sign,
And anyone selling loose meat ba's,
Is liable tae a fine.

That's why it's possible nooadays
Tae roam this pleasant land,
Withoot treading on a loose meat ba',
For loose meat ba's are banned.
And though these dreadful days,
Are gone and far awa',
You'll find it doon in history books
As the year o' the great beef ba'.

(Genus Corvus) Can I just draw your attention to the Latin phrase in this next poem or song. The phrase is Genus Corvus and is Latin for the family of crows. I hope this will be apparent at the end of the poem.

THE NOSE-BLAW SONG

With feeling.

There's a wee hoose 'mang the heather
Where we used tae sit and blether,
And ma Granny wore her sandshoes a' the while.
She sat up wi' her tranni did ma dear auld fashioned Granny,
For she wis aufy bothered wi' the bile.
But we'll be unco merry when she loups aff Renfrew Ferry
And greets us in the Paki's at the Cross,
And we'll eat oor Indian curries and forget auld Scotia's worries,
Then we'll sing some Scottish songs and get morose.

Chorus:
Ah love ma Granny, ma boney Hielan' Granny,
Though she's auld and wrinkled like a prune,
But Ah'll still love ma Granny, ma Granny wi' her tranni,
Though sometimes her knickers fa' right doon.

There's a wee hoose 'mang the heather,
Where Ah got a skelpit leather',
When Granny caught me wi' Kirsty in the byre.
But Ah'll be marching back along yon heather track,
Tae the purple hills that blossom near Strathyre.

36

Wi' a fish supper in ma sporran Ah'll march tae early morn
Till Ah see the wee hoose Ah desire,
Then Ah'll hae a plateful porridge flavoured wi' sweet
borage,
But first turn at the oak tree near Strathyre.

Then we'll wander in the gloamond
On the slopes of big Ben Lomond,
Before Ah don ma boots and head tae Luss,
And wi' soup stains oan ma broo, Ah'll say, "Ta-ta the noo,
Ah'll have tae shoot the craw." (Genus Corvus).

The expression, "Tae shoot the craw", is a peculiarly Scottish one and
describes a person who wishes to disappear very quickly.

Bridal Night

EPITAPHS

COWBOY'S EPITAPH

The blow was fatal, even severe,
When he collided with a runaway steer.

EPITAPH FROM A SLENDER WOMAN
TO HER HUSBAND

I'll always miss you, darling,
You came in handy when we ate,
For anything I couldn't finish,
You scoffed right off my plate.

CABINET MAKER

A worker in all sorts of wood,
He would have stayed if he could.
He left his loving wife and wean,
Much though it went against the grain.

WINDOW CLEANER

You cleaned the panes so nice and bright,
It showed the cobwebs in the light.
You had no time to wave your shammy
Before you left your grieving Mammy.

ELLEN MACPHEE

This stone erected by J.S. MacPhee,
In memory of his daughter.
A memorial to him it could well be,
It was the only thing he bought her.

AN ORDINARY BLOKE

One thing worries me up here,
And has now for some time.
On earth I spoke like an ordinary bloke,
But here I speak in rhyme.

STREET SWEEPER

He swept up snaw in freezing cauld,
Was found frozen tae the bone.
The doctor gave the fatal cause —
Forgot to put his Long John's oan.

A GARDENER'S BELOVED HORSE

It's many a year since you plodded off,
To that stable in the skies,
It's many a year since the rhubarb grew,
And the rose is now shrunken in size.

BUS DRIVER

The gates of Heaven opened wide,
The Angels quickly jumped aside,
As he raced past the waiting queue,
Which, after all, was nothing new.

OLD PLUMBERS

What happens to old plumbers
When their life draws to an end?
They keep looking for forgotten tools,
And end up roon' the bend.

DOBBIN'S EPITAPH

Alas, poor Dobbin your song is sung,
You're not required likewise your dung.
A blade of grass and you worked all day,
And if it was withered a blade of hay.
Often you've pulled the heavy plough,
A sight we don't see often now.
How painful then were your swollen hocks,
Which would have benefited by warm, woolly socks.
But the farmer was more interested in corn,
And treated both horse and wife with scorn.
I hear you hated him when you were livin'.
But up in Heaven you'll be forgiven.
You'll be looked after, gentle Dobbin,
For when your swollen hocks are throbbin'
The angels will really do you proud
And bandage your feet with lumps of cloud.

RETIRED STOKER

My fire went out, I had to go,
But really I am lucky,
Not to be in Hell below,
With my hands forever mucky .

PUBLICAN

It's not so bad up here at all,
In fact, at times, we have a ball.
We play our harps when duty's done,
And theres plenty spirits for everyone .

A DOUBLE-GLAZING SALESMAN

There's not much I can do up here,
In fact it's so amazing,
With only angels playing harps,
There's no need for double-glazing

A BURGLAR

He crept in to a public house,
When the light grew dim,
And was picking a padlock
When the Lord picked him.

A VETERINARY SURGEON

He loved animals all his life,
More perhaps, than his dear wife,
Who, being of a forgiving nature,
Helped him with each sickly crature .

A BEAT CONSTABLE

A well known constable on his beat,
His last words to his wife were sweet.
"I leave you now without a doubt,
That is all — Over and Out!"

A GIRL NAMED ROSE

Gone from us is a faded flower,
A life of sunshine and seldom a shower.
The end came sudden — the diagnose,
Blockage of greenfly up her nose.

AN OLD CLOCKMAKER

Your chimes are silent now here you lie
With your main spring broke.
Your feet have stopped at half-past six
And your hands at twelve o'clock.

AN OLD SAUSAGE MAKER

A sausage maker all his days,
We remember him fondly over drinks.
A friend he was to all of us,
Till the severing of his links.

PARTICIPANT IN THE HIGHLAND GAMES

He tossed the mighty caber,
It was a mighty throw.
He tossed the mighty caber
But forgot to let it go.

REVEREND THOMAS CUMMING

A good man lies beneath this stone,
The Reverend Thomas Cummin',
Who loved his fellow men,
Likewise his fellow wummen.

He raced to help his fellow men,
This nimble-footed Pastor,
But, alas, he wasn't quick enough
For death came somewhat faster.

FIREWORK MAKER

Two years to go before he retired,
He lit the blue touch paper and then he expired.

TELEPHONIST

Suddenly you were called away
And left us all alone.
We never heard that fatal call,
For we do not have a 'phone.

A KEEN GARDENER

Here you lie transplanted,
Your growing season's ended.
But like your cabbage you'll be to us
Highly recommended.

FAMILY COOK

You left your recipes to us,
Like your famous Irish Stew.
When we have heartburn after dinner,
'Tis then we think of you.

CAPTAIN OF A TUG OF WAR TEAM

Here lies James Adams,
Once strong as a bull.
But not strong enough
To resist the Lord's pull.

ROBERT HALL GLUTTON

Rab Ha' gorged himself on food,
The end it came quite sudden.
Efter four meat pies, a pun' o' ham,
And a daud o' mealy pudden.

JAMES MELLOR COFFEE GRINDER

He was grinding coffee when the trumpet sounded,
Now like his beans the grinder's grounded.

MAGICIAN

Here today and gone the next,
Not one of his repeated tricks.

CATS

The howling cats at eventide,
How they get my wick.
I wish that I among them were
With a heavy, bliddy stick.

A JOINER

He fretted for his departed wife,
He fretted long and weary.
But noo he'll fret no more this life,
For now he's joined his dearie.

ANOTHER JOINER

A working joiner all his life,
Who sometimes joined his brother.
Now, though he's left his tools behind,
He's gone to join his brother.

ODDS AND ENDS

POOR GRANNY

Homeward Granny in winter goes,
Frozen fingers and frozen toes.
Ballasted with shopping bags of plastic.
Knickers hanging — burst elastic.

A LOVING MUM

The window glass now sparkles bright,
A hand moves a moistened shammy.
The hand belongs to a loving mum,
For she is someone's mammy.

A HEN-PECKED MAN

I know a wee, hen-pecked man,
Whose eyes held a hopeful gleam,
When he gave his wife a present,
A jar of vanishing cream.

BEWARE

Beware, ye scorners of my verse,
Do not be sarcastic.
Ere I load my catapult,
The one with strong elastic!

CATTLE IN WINTRY WOODS

I implore ye one and all,
To think of the coos who are not in a stall,
But are outside on a cold, wintry day,
Groaning in a most pathetic way.

With splinters of ice stuck in their muzzle,
A result of trying frozen grass to guzzle.
The animals snuffle at the ice-bound frozen leaves,
Which could have gave them shelter had they no' fell aff
the trees .

So any time you are eating beef or wee meat balls,
Think of the beasts who are not in nice stalls.
And if, by chance, you have a bundle of hay,
Hasten doon tae the coos right away.

THE GARDEN GNOME Unabridged.

Have you thought of the poor gnome in winter,
His whiskers all froze to his jerkin,
With his cap a target for vandals
And his nose like a wee, pickled gherkin?
His brows hang heavy and hoary with frost,
Both his eyes are hidden from view,
His nose glows red in the darkness
And both his big toes are blue.

When swallows depart in the autumn,
The wee garden gnomes are the losers,
Neglected and covered wi' auld rotten leaves
And their bums hinging oot o' their troosers.
It's degrading for the wee gnome in winter,
When hungry, wee birds are aboot,
His chest is festooned wi' peanuts,
Hauf a coconut hings fae his snoot.

But hearken! The spring it hath sprungeth,
From his nose an icicle drops,
It pierces its way through his troosers
And skewers his feet to his socks.
Yes! Spring comes with snowdrops a' gleaming,
In the apple trees rises the sap,
And rabbits who should know better,
Do dreadful things in his lap.

He dreams of catching huge goldfish,
He's been dreaming and fishing some time,
His patience is really remarkable,
For there's no bait on the end of his line.
The birds are cheerfully whistling
On the branches just overhead,
And his cap that used to be crimson
Is crimson with white spots instead.

At times the bees from the bee-hive,
Confused by the scent of a rose,
Crash-land upon his white whiskers,
And seek nectar far up his red nose.
These wee bees tickle his nostrils
And cause the poor fella tae sneeze,
There's a noise like a crazy machine-gun
As he sneezes oot hunners o' bees.

He complains of things maist uncanny,
Of things uncannily weird,
Like a wasp's nest in his semmit
And a wren's nest built in his beard.
You'll maybe feel pangs of pity,
As you hear him rant and curse,
But don't take him home to the telly,
For the telly, at times, is far worse.

THE GARDEN GNOME 2

But one dusk a fairy on gossamer wing,
Appeared wi' fairy-like chuckles,
The gnome's eyes popped — doon hung his jaw,
And whiter turned his knuckles.
A pain like a red hot needle
Ran through his wee shaking knees,
Could this be love or rheumatics
Or maybe just stings from the bees?

She lingered a while so enchanting,
In her see-through goon o' silk,
And he could see her wee body,
As white as the pussy cat's milk.
He yearned for that wee female fairy,
As she giggled and danced through the wood,
Evil thoughts tortured his body,
If only he could — then he would!

49

As he watched that fluttering fairy,
A shudder ran through his wee vest,
If only he could clasp that wee fairy,
Just once to his wee plastic chest.
Wi' a heart as big as a marra,
And likewise stuffed wi' love,
He cried oot tae that wee fairy,
"Aw hen, you've dropped your glove!"

She sat herself doon o' so coyly,
On the shaft o' the garden barra,
And her eyes were full of promise
And quite a lot of mascara.
A tremor shot through his wee body,
And he stiffly turned his head,
First to the beautiful fairy
And thence to the potting shed.

Oh, that night was so full of wonder,
Amidst scent fae the flowers so sweet,
When the gnome staggered oot the next morning,
His wellies were on the wrang feet.
The elves, when they heard, held a meeting,
They were jealous but shouted, "Disgrace!"
But that wee gnome just sat there,
Wi' a silly, big grin on his face.

Each morning the wee gnome still sits there,
As if he was under a spell,
Wi' steam pouring oot o' his wellies
And his toes turning up as well.
Then he dozes as waits for the gloaming,
And he dreams of his fairy, "wee Mary",
Of her smile like a spring morning
And her oxters so wonderful hairy.

JUVENILE DAYS

Oh the soup that mother made,
By the candle's feeble glow,
Globules of grease 'mang the steaming peas
And the marrow-bone clean as snow.

Oh yon days of the hungry time,
When your spine said hello to your belly.
Oh yon days of raggy breeks,
When naebody had a telly.

Oh yon days o' the Highland Dancing,
Oh the sound of the Pibroch's wheeze.
Oh the shy and cautious glancing
At the flashing female knees.

BONNY BARE-LEGGED BESSIE

She wore a tartan tammy,
And a tartan skirt brand new,
And because she sat too near the fire
Her legs were tartan too.

WARNING

A woman when on holiday,
A woman no longer young,
Was treated by a doctor,
For sunburn on her tongue.

POETICAL FEVER

Oh cool my fevered brow with ice
And thereon place a slice
Of corned beef or maybe two,
Then I shall sleep for an hour or two.

Then awaken with my headache gone
And feast upon that slice of corn,
Cooked and crisped to a high degree
Accompanied by a pot of tea.

Then I could lie like Rip Van Winkle,
With corn beef crumbs in every wrinkle,
Whilst giving a reassuring stroke,
To the five pound note stuffed in my sock.

CHURCH COLLECTION

I put five pence into the bowl,
Then carefully looked about.
Nobody was watching me —
So I took a fiver out.

THE KOOKABURRA

I ponder on the Kookaburra,
Had a rabbit been its mother,
Would it be a Rabbitburra?
And as I cannot be more thurra,
I leave this problem to annurra,
The ever-probing Attenborough.

CONSERVATION

The russet gold of a sunbeam,
Strikes through the woodland bold,
And shines upon the gusset
Of old knickers green with mould.

The thrilling trilling of a blackbird's song,
Is halted by a cough as he inhales the pong
Of burning tyres and smouldering clothes,
Which moist the eye and titillate the nose.

Near where a herd of foxes take their ease,
Sharing food and each others fleas,
In leafy green mysterious vaults,
Lie empty bottles — Vodka, Gin and various malts.

A rabbit slides by in stealthy guile,
Helped by paws coated in Diesel ile.
A starling whose feet is thick wi' grease,
Fails to grasp some slippery cheese.

The gold-eyed toad with quivering jaw,
A fly grasped tightly in warty paw,
A bottle thrown, a sudden gulp,
Both fly and toad a sodden pulp.

Oh conservationists heed our pleas,
Where would we hide our waste if there were no trees?
Preserve the woodland which encompasses a',
Hiding garbage both from man and flying craw.

THE CHAIR

Maist poets get their pleasure
Fae beauty everywhere,
But tae me there's greater pleasure
Just relaxing on a chair.

When life is fu' o' hardship,
When life is fu' o' care,
There's still a wee bit comfort
Just dozing on a chair.

Just dreaming o' the good times,
Of times beyond compare,
Of true friends and happiness
In your comfy chair.

And though the springs are flattened,
And your bum is near the flair,
You're nearer noo tae Heaven
In your auld arm chair!

WINTER MORNING IN THE SUBURBS

Winter has came the land is destitute,
Upon the bare apple trees there is no fruit,
And little birds must the icy wind beware,
Lest it blow their feathers off and leave them bare.

The entire land is white with snow,
And chilblain sufferers cry, "Oh! Oh! Oh!"
At dawn there's groans and sleepers stirring
And the forlorn sound of car engines whirring.

Until there comes a very loud shout,
And the housewife leaves her corn flakes and looks out,
And louder still the cry of pain,
As her good man kicks their car again and again.

For the car does not understand his curses or pleas,
For like nine out of ten it is Japanese.
And starving wee birds lie claws uppermost,
For these are the ones who have gave up the ghost.

Both Robin, Duck and drab Hedge Sparrow.
Are frozen stiff unto the marrow.
Icy snow crackles underfoot
And the Owl no longer gives a hoot.

At times my heart is heavy when I think of poor, old Joe,
Who was called to Heaven but left his barra doon below.
Yet still his cry's resounding, resounding in my ears,
"My peers is nice and juicy, "Wha'll buy my Honey Peers?"

Wi' various fruits and size ten boots he stood for many years,
Begging doubtful shoppers to try his Honey Peers.
His barra stood forenenst the kerb fae Morn to Dark o'clock,
And his left foot was frozen cauld for he had but one good sock.

I visualize with baith ma eyes poor Joseph doon the years,
As he wi' right foot forward cries, "Wha'll buy my Honey Peers?"
Aye, when dreary was the Wintry day and red raw your frozen ears,
Your thoughts were drawn to a cheery fire and a plate of Honey Peers.

And when Spring came a'louping in and blew the snaw awa',
It was great tae sook some Honey Peers, especially wi' your Maw.
Wi' juice bubbling fae each one, how succulent they be!
A slice of melon may be nice but the seeds get in your e'e.

Friends, tread softly ower Joseph's grave lest the ghost of
him appears,
And through the gloom, in vain implores, "Wha'll buy my
Honey Peers?"
Dismal and dark is now his plot all overgrown wi' weeds,
But underfoot, "Be careful there!" are sprouting wee peer
seeds.

And later when the trees have grown and the Honey Peers
are swelling,
The green leaves as they wave above will shade poor
Joseph's dwelling.
I'm happy now but a bit red-eyed, how whisky draws the
tears!
When I think of Joe's upturned toes, Ah, a Peer among his
Peers.

SEEKING SOLACE 'NEATH A TREE

Oft my memrie takes me back,
To when I roamed the countryside.
Where bluebells near the railway track
Waved to their fellows on either side.

Now ancient sleepers lie asleep,
For trains no longer pass
And meadow flowers shyly peep,
Through green and tangled grass.

And dull-eyed sheep with shaggy hips,
Their chewing jaws slip side to side,
Enclosing sweet clover with their lips,
While vaguely viewing the countryside.

Oft 'neath the beech's mighty span,
Far from life's unending clamour.
I'd introduce my frying pan
To an egg or perhaps a banger.

Then with my dog I'd take my pause
And listen to his belly rumble,
As he watched my moving jaws,
Till pacified by apple crumble.

WINTER WOODLAND

Come with me I implore all ye who may,
To see a Winter Woodland upon a Winter's day.
Come thou who slumps in slothful ease,
His vest a collage of breakfast bacon, egg and grease.
What carest thou or even thine
About the fate of frozen, huddled kine?
Who should be snug and warm in farmer's byre,
Not knee-deep in hoof-marked, freezing mire.
But I advise ye who are otherwise ill and therefore not able,
To erect outside a wooden bird-table.
This gives ye all a chance to see
Wild birds in comfort as ye sup your tea.

Come friends, and wonder at that tiny morsel the
  Jenny Wren,
Flitting mouse-like in its icy den.
I often think on this feathered mite and suppose,
Were it human it would have a dewdrop on its nose.
Sometimes the wild wind dislodges a beechnut from the
highest beech,
Which descends rapidly and strikes the wren, which gives
a screech.

Which would be the equivalent of "Ouch!" in the human speech.
Also observe the fox in this cruel, silent winter,
Devour a woodmouse skewered by an icy splinter.
'Twas the warmth of a sudden thaw,
Which despatched an icicle from a tree, 'tis nature's law,
And pierced the woodmouse through heart and paw.

Yet some who come may shout with contorted, purple face,
"See them beer cans — a dam disgrace!"
When they view a former pretty place.
Which no longer presents to the eye a sight full of allure,
Except, perhaps, to the eye of a greedy brewer.
But I can assure them in the summer of next year, without fear,
Mother Nature will hide the rusty cans outline,
With assorted wild flowers including the Lesser Celandine.
But hark! The silence is enhanced by the croaking of a solitary crow,
Basking in the feeble warmth of the sun's morning glow,
Or it might well be a rook,
It's difficult to tell without a second look.

But nothing is more calculated to set the feeding rabbit's teeth on edge,
As eating a frozen mouthful from the frozen rush-like sedge.
Each little leaf encased in icy, glass-like sheath,
Makes the poor rabbit cringe and grit his trembling, yellow teeth.
And as I return by the bonnie banks of Clyde,
I note cormorants fishing which signifies the water is now purified.

For many times in the past I've seen drowned dogs floating by,
Which even to the manliest of men would bring a tear to his eye.
Floating by with four legs erect and bloated belly distended,
Now, thanks to the Lord and the Purification Board this is now ended.

And I'll never forget the beseeching beech with mighty arms silhouetted,
A sight, which to his day, I have not regretted.
And likewise the steaming green patches of grass where the sun has been,
Thereby stirring the poet's emotions, especially in his spleen.
So, I hope by this message I have encouraged ye all,
To go out in the winter or, as they say in America, the late, late Fall.

THE DANDELION

Oh bright, sun-shaped yella floo'er,
Growing in hot Summer's stoor.
In the grun' there's no' a bit of nourishment,
Yet here you are and here you are content.

I trust you and yet your kinfolk make a mockery,
By invading my carefully planned Alpine rockery.
Thrusting forth their yella sun-shaped heids
And joining forces with other obnoxious weeds.

And against the freshly-painted garden gate,
A stray dug feels the need to urinate.
His careless owner can't deny where he's been,
For under his right hand hind leg is a patch of green.

Is it worth it? I say to masel',
Is it worth it? Is it Hell!
Is it worth it a' this digging?
Is it worth it? You must be kidding.

A PLOUGHMAN'S COTTAGE

By Edgar's lonely cottage door,
Where midgies jostle by the score,
Oft I sit from morn till night,
To watch these innocents in flight.

Oft sat I in solitude.
Admiring with both my eyes
A swarm of hungry ladybirds,
A brace of butterflies.

And when the farmer counts his yield
Of turnips from his turnip field
It gives me pleasure, now and then,
To share an oatcake with a hen.

RA GAZEBO

There's so many interests to help us relax,
Away from the farm the office, telex and fax.
City Bar Yuppies relax between retchings,
Caused by gulping tottie crisps likewise port scretchings.
And malcontents dream of ladies wielding whips,
And skelping them on buttocks or hairy hips.

Though I do not grudge these folk their hour of doubtful pleasure,
I have other ways in which to spend my leisure.
For I love the simpler things of life,
Like a wee, fried sausage, preferably sliced.
And I invite selected friends to see my Gazebo
Which I made out of my own head and in which striped
tomatoes, (Tigerella), grow.

My friends gaze at the Gazebo, which they admire,
And wonder how I could both these skills acquire,
A Poet and Gazebo Designer as well!
And, let's face it, they are as jealous as Hell!
For it is beyond human or even female ken,
That some are born poets and others only men.

"But hark to me," I say, "Gentle wummen and fellow men,
The poet Byron did not become famous until he invented
the ball-point pen!"
For I will be remembered ere I go,
Both as Poet and Designer of Gazebo,
Even the great Charles Rennie Mac.,
With all the experience at his back,
Never dared, as far as I know,
To design a common or garden Gazebo.

Then whiles I tread the streets and observe the few,
Who stagger around and spoil the view
Their mates are there also, sublimely supine,
The potholes a' fitting the curve of their spine.
But what I find is sadly amiss,
When they settle discussions with the famed Glasgow kiss.

Then when pubs are shut and punters *palely loitering**,
After regurgitating curry suppers, the penalty for unwise
roistering,
It's time to go hame to my wee Butt and Ben,
Two goats I keep in an outside pen.

Though real poets aspire to mansions and palaces,
I sit, *Al Fresco,** content in my *Galluses,**,
Listening to wee birds as they sing,
Their cheeks puffed oot like anything.
Or I can repair to my Gazebo, therein to take my ease,
Undisturbed by journalists who descend like myriads of
fleas.

I have provided a translation of the more difficult foreign words and
phrases, galluses for example.

'palely loitering' John Keats 1795 — 1821. Who invented flea powder,
I believe.
From La Belle Dame Sans Merci (Fr). Mercy oan us, Auntie Bella's still
wearing they auld sandshoes! (Gla).

Al Fresco (It). In the garden.

Galluses (Gla). Suspenders (Amer). Usually worn at the trail, as it is
sometimes awkward for pensioners to fasten them to socks.

Motto: My Destiny is in the lap of the Goats.

BIOGRAPHICAL NOTES

After leaving school at fourteen McCorrisken became, in turn, an apprentice upholsterer, a shipyard labourer, an aircraft worker and a gravedigger before being called to defend his country.

He has vivid memories of his basic army training. Rather than labour through the intricacies of a map reference to pinpoint an enemy position, little drawings were used, i.e., Bushy-top Tree, position 3 o'clock.

The sergeant constantly bawling these simple instructions to the new recruits.

The silence of the barrack room night was frequently broken by a restless sleeper mumbling, 'Bushy-top Tree, 3 o'clock.', which triggered off a drowsy chorus of, 'Ivy-clad Clock Tower, 9 o'clock.'
These exchanges went on until dawn.

Luckily during his army career McCorrisken encountered very few bushy-topped trees and none at 3 o'clock. Had he been posted to the Western Desert he could easily have become deranged.

After being discharged from the army he obtained a situation as a swine herd.

Sundays, the pigs were taken to the butcher's. At times it was difficult to get the reluctant pigs into the large van. One Sunday the head man handed McCorrisken a torch like object.
'It gives them a wee electric shock.' he said. 'We'll have them aboard in no time.'

When the pigs were prodded the charge was apparently too powerful, for the squealing beasts took off vertically and headed for the hills.
McCorrisken is still convinced that there is a race of straight-tailed pigs inhabiting a remote Highland glen.

Further frustrations followed until he entered a bad poetry competition run by the then Glasgow Herald which he won "by a country mile." Since then he has captivated a wider audience by his television recitations.

The cumulative result of his experiences is this nostalgic, vivid portrayal of country life in which one can almost catch a whiff of farm horse and ferret. He has put his finger on Mother Nature's pulse and plucked her heart strings.

Now, as oak and beech are being butchered and the countryside depleted he is arguably the last of the great rural bards.